Hundred Block
ROCK

Bud Osborn

ARSENAL PULP PRESS
Vancouver

ARSENAL PULP PRESS
103-1014 Homer Street
Vancouver, BC Canada V6B 2W9
www.arsenalpulp.com

 The publisher gratefully acknowledges the support of the
Canada Council for the Arts and the B.C. Arts Council for its
publishing program.

Canadä The publisher gratefully acknowledges the support of the
Government of Canada through the Book Publishing Industry
Development Program for its publishing activities.

Typeset by the Vancouver Desktop Publishing Centre
Author photograph by Barry Peterson and
Blaise Enright-Peterson
Printed and bound in Canada

CANADIAN CATALOGUING IN PUBLICATION DATA

Osborn, Bud, 1947-.
Hundred block rock

Poems.

ISBN 1-55152-074-5
I. Title.
PS8579.S33H86 1999   C811'54.   C99-910729-1
PR9199.3.O78H86 1999

table of contents

"poetry is about telling the truth"

—JUNE JORDAN

Since no human being accomplishes anything alone, I dedicate this collection of poems to the many people who literally kept me alive through the years when I had lost all caring for myself. In a very profound sense, this book is a collaboration.

amazingly alive

here I am
amazingly alive
tried to kill myself twice
by the time I was five
sometimes it's hard to take one more breath
inside this north american
culture of death

big big trouble
from the time I was born
lots of people get stripped
right to the bone
say nobody's gonna
touch me anymore
if I'm gonna live
gonna be a cutthroat whore
can't touch my heart
can't touch my soul
yeah I know all about
this north american
culture of horror

but here we are
amazingly alive
against long odds
left for dead
lazarus couldn't have been
more shocked than me
to have been brought back
from the dead

a judge told me
I was of no use

no use at all
to society
but I got news
news for him
a society of bullshit
bullshit and greed
ain't no damn use
ain't no use to me

this hotshot head shrink
at a locked-up nuthouse
told me I was so
totally hopeless
so far out
and so fucked up
nothing could ever
wake my life up
but I got news for him
today
I'm so amazingly alive
I'm dancin
dancin on my own grave

had knives at my throat
thrown from a car had my back broke
gun pointed at my heart
lay bleedin to death
in a dark city park
been o.d.ed so bad made a doctor mad
lookin at me said
you're still alive
how can that be?
said I don't know why I'm alive except I don't want to be
but I got news
for that doctor too
right now I'm so alive

repetition to emphasize. [handwritten annotation]

feelin so free
doctor your science ain't nothin
behind this
mystery

so here we are
amazingly alive
against long odds
and left for dead
inside a culture teachin ten thousand ways
ways to die
before we're dead
but here we are
amazingly alive

I used to hate it
hate
hate wakin up
say not another damn day shit make it all go away
woke up one day
wearin a straitjacket
locked in a padded cell
thought I was dead and buried
deep in hell
but today I woke up
sayin got me one more
one more day never thought I'd have before

so I'm dancin
first thing
this brand new morning
dancin first thing
to otis redding
dancin with a woman
in my arms
naked in the sunshine

naked in the breeze
these arms of mine
wrapped around her
lord have mercy
her arms around me

I used to wake up
so low and mean
so down and out
wake up most days now
I say shout
shout with my heart
and shout with my eyes
shout with my balls
and shout with my feet
shout with my fingers
and shout with my soul
shout for life
more abundantly
shout for all
hard-pressed messed-with human beings
shout my last breath
shout fuck this north american culture of death

had to stop runnin
face my pain
stop killin myself
face my pain
my pain was lightning
comin down like rain
but facin me
only way I found
to start gettin free
gettin free of north america
inside of me

gettin free of this death culture
drivin me

so here I am
here we are
amazingly alive
against long odds
left for dead
north america tellin lies
in our head
make you feel like shit
better off dead

so most days now
I say shout
shout for joy
shout for love
shout for you
shout for us
shout down this system
puts our souls in prison

say shout for life
shout with our last breath
shout fuck this north american culture of death

shout here we are
amazingly alive
against long odds
left for dead
shoutin this death culture
dancin this death culture
out of our heads

amazingly alive

toledo blues

unholy toledo

renamed today by graffiti
on grey walls and t-shirts
ZERO CITY
where the spirit of tecumseh
drifts above the poisoned maumee river
where police discover
satanic mutilations and blood-altars

unholy toledo

a burned-out laid-off radiation-cancer-zone
my hometown

indescribably happy for a moment at least
my grandmother's preserved photographic proof
an ordinary advertisement for kodak camera
displayed in the only local newspaper
I was a chubby child with curly blond hair
running head-long and ecstatic
towards the outstretched arms of my mother
my father kneeling nearby
aiming a camera to record a successful domestic image
the message obvious
BE LIKE THIS FAMILY

be like this city
toledo ohio in 1950
a paragon of prosperity
in the wealthiest and most powerful nation
in the history of the world

today near the end of the second millennium
I see boarded-up and broken-into blocks of houses
entire vacated smashed-up neighbourhoods
empty hotels and deserted factories
new soup kitchens and emergency shelters
long foodbank line-ups and welfare cutbacks
a tent city for refugees within zero city

crack cocaine out of control
solid citizens and politicians calling for martial law
and euthanasia
for increasing numbers of crack-addict babies

where posters on city buses proclaim collapse
"if you use a .38 in a robbery
it's a mandatory 5 years
have you got school problems?
call this number
have you got family problems?
alcohol-drug-disease-suicide-pregnancy problems?
call this number"
crimestoppers reward posters
TURN IN YOUR NEIGHBOUR FOR MONEY
and neighbourhood watch signs
over every terrorized street sign

where the long ago happy kodak family
has long since been destroyed
where the local newspaper printed an editorial
one year after the kodak ad
condemning my family as an example of
"the consequences of flaunting contempt
for the moral laws on which
our society ultimately rests"

full-page sensational suicide and sex scandal
the message obvious
DON'T BE LIKE THIS FAMILY
my father hanged himself in jail
my mother went crazy and tried to kill herself
my aunt shot my grandmother in the heart
and turned the gun on herself

unholy toledo

where
my friends
koontz burned alive in a drunken gas heater fireball
louanne was beaten and raped and dumped in a cemetery
maureen slashed her wrists
amy drove her car with her daughter in it
to the middle of railroad tracks
and waited for the train
where morningstar staggered out of a bar on lagrange street
and fell beneath the wheels of a truck
where my closest childhood friend robin ehret
murdered himself
where lance smith blew his head apart
with his father's shotgun in the family bathroom
where preston blount froze to death in a downtown alley
where ray logan froze to death on the sidewalk
in front of the salvation army
where sammi owens froze to death in an abandoned storefront
and his namesake steals for food
and spends his youth in jail
where I lived in a halfway house for drunken bums
with retarded billy rogers
who sodomized and strangled a little girl
in zero city

toledo ohio

where a mugger pulped my friend donald bond's brain
with a 2–by–4
and where helen who lived downstairs on western avenue
smeared her face with a dead dog's blood and foam
and whose mother pulled her own hair out
in bloody clumps

where my closest high school friends and myself
lived on the same residential avenue
jim's mother drank herself to death in her 50s
tom's mother had nervous breakdowns
and overdosed on pills
dying in her 40s
chuck's mother started crying and couldn't stop
or set the table for invisible guests
so she'd have someone to talk to
and received another psych ward confinement
and tranquilizers
but their houses were neat and clean
they were usually smiling
and wearing cosmetics carefully applied
none of them knew of the others' anguish
though their husbands' business careers thrived
on berdan-avenue-in-hell
in zero city

where my uncle earl fought scabs and police
and the u.s. army
organizing unions
until he died from alcohol poisoning
where my grandfather les died young
of childhood coal-mine black lung
and my other grandfather died a drunk and a bum

where my friend george love's brother
hanged himself in a boxcar
where louie holloway the wino artist
lost his toes from exposure
where billy and bobby devlin
my little dearborn-avenue-next-door-5-year-old-friends
became a brutal drunk and a convict junkie
respectively
where my good friend danny stole a truck
on his way to kill his father
who'd beaten and tortured him as a child
but was arrested first and turned 18 in prison
where my mother father uncle stepfather
ex-wife and myself
were locked up in the same downtown jail
at different times for different crimes
where omar my arab roommate
just out of prison from the civil war in beirut
shot a biker coming after him with a broken bottle
calmly in the head 4 times
in brenda's body shop

where my friend jeffrey the body builder
who used to bring me protein powder
murdered a man in cold blood and bragged about it
and is now doing life for homicide
where dewey blanchard who could recite by heart
"the hound of heaven"
was thrown from a car with his throat cut

unholy toledo

where my friend paulette picked up syphilis turning tricks
and was thrown by her pimp from a 2nd-storey window
breaking her back and paralyzing her

her pimp a guy named eddie
my basketball-playing buddy

toledo ohio

where the valedictorian of my high school class
mixed a lethal poison and left a note saying
"I'm tired"
where my friend beverly a lesbian
heard voices telling her to stab a man
and she did stick him 14 times
and did 10 years in prison

zero city
originally called
THE BLACK SWAMP

where charlie shipman
a short smart-ass joker with one dead arm
who showed me the ropes in a local institution
was eaten by rats
beneath a black velvet billboard
in the weeds beside the river
on summit street

where archie an old friend of my mother and father
was beaten to death in the tavern he owned
by somebody who said he just wanted to take a piss
where ray ray's mother in the south end
sold blowjobs in their living room
and ray ray's eyes at 7 years old
looked hard as sonny liston's in the ring

where doctor fisch a psychiatrist
at the toledo mental health centre

the nuthouse
told me I was "emotionally disturbed"
then said "the world is going to end in cannibalism"

the black swamp

where doctor bitar
a sociologist at toledo university
declared to me that
"what america is becoming will make hitler's germany
look like a sunday school picnic"

unholy toledo

where I was locked up with eric
a vietnam vet who had explosions going off in his head
and was afraid he was going to hurt someone
and locked up with gary
who went through vietnam without a scratch
but back home in toledo
was shot in the stomach by his girlfriend
where my long-time friend joyce
hallucinates thieves breaking into her locked-up life

toledo ohio

where I sold my blood at the plasma centre
sold my muscles in warehouses
sold my sex for money

where my friend joe piasecki
who lifted my spirit despite myself
became superintendent of schools
and was shot to death
by a teacher who resented him

where crysta
a woman I've known for years
tried to sell her baby in a bar for a drink
and was arrested for it
where my friend bill
janitor of the downtown ymca
was stabbed fatally
mopping the hallway
his killer found naked and on his knees
praying in the lobby

the black swamp

where the only person I've ever trusted enough
to collapse in tears in his arms
a tough guy from the north end
an organized crime guy
my stepfather louie
who never harmed me
was convicted of raping a 9-year-old girl
and is doing 6 to 25 years
in the penitentiary

unholy toledo

where 20 years ago
I walked into southwyck shopping mall
and read a sign above a video arcade saying
CREATE YOUR OWN REALITY
I knew what it meant
another invitation to death

zero city

where when drunk one night
fell backwards against a concrete curb
cracking my skull open
and crawled into the wet grass and shadows
of scott park at 3:30 in the morning
blood pumping out of an artery
a police car passed near but didn't see me
I gave up
I was dying and glad of it
but a white cadillac appeared in the street
strong arms lifted me to my feet
placed me drunk bleeding and muddy
into a clean backseat
pressed a white towel to my head
my anonymous samaritans
brought me back from the dead
drove me to toledo hospital
where still alive and resentful
I believed my life
meaningless evil

toledo ohio

where the head of psychology
at toledo state mental hospital
pronounced me "hopeless"

unholy toledo

where in the middle of the afternoon one summer day so-
ber a few weeks walking down erie street rush hour traffic blasting
I was given a moment that changed life for me
I'd believe the moment changed me but that it'd take
many years much suffering before I was willing to stop running
face myself and allow the upheavals of real change to occur

I'd simply looked at a gnarled and diseased old tree limbs sawn-off yet a branch or 2 grew sprouting new life green leaves

and heard a sound like forests of leaves singing in a fierce wind a wind flooding that cold and insatiable hole in my gut with joy pure joy

I looked around at automobiles buildings trash in the gutter other people on the street and an indisputable certainty informed me 'everything is all right'

and for a man formerly and fervently convinced everything details relationships circumstances of daily and my life and life itself hopelessly wrong this revelation contradicted experience

yet the deaths violence madness not the final word but inexplicably within them and through them everything is all right everything sheer joy embracing all appearances to the contrary in a oneness of joy each thing distinctive yet wedded in joy

and THIS is who and what I am beyond experiences of death and deeper than condemnations and negations

THIS PRODIGIOUS AFFIRMATION

I resumed walking down erie street towards a residence for women alcoholics where my wife worked and when I entered the front door she started toward me but halted mid-way her face changing expression like a kaleidoscope adjusting to bring coloured stones into focus and finally said "what happened to you?"

holy toledo

jazz after midnight
along granville street

TO GRAHAM ORD

a saxophone moans on granville street

two little white boys sit on the sidewalk
knees pulled up under their chins

a mournful solo after midnight

there's a man standing in the middle of the block
he holds a telephone in one hand
and in the other
                a long knife
                        jabbing
                                against his heart
        a long knife
                        jabbing
                                against his heart

saxophone solo on granville street

chilly   after midnight   blues   so
                                        deep

cops arrive   draw their guns

the man drops the phone   but clutches that knife

he screams "don't move!"   and a dozen cops freeze

and a saxophone floats   above granville street

I say "lord have mercy   have mercy please!"

(handwritten: 어버지, 지네가요 사랑?)

more cruisers slide on up   red lights flashing

(handwritten: stopped cars.)

the buses are   backed up

a cop shouts "get in a doorway!
                go to the end of the block!"

he's clearing the scene

(handwritten: long, loud high-pitched cries which express sorrow & pain 울부짖다)

and a saxophone (wails)   on granville street
weaving through a cold (tableau) *(handwritten: scene, picture)*
of a man in trouble   a crowd   and police

a gunshot   POP!

(handwritten: very)
(handwritten: walks unsteadily)

and the man   drilled   (staggers) a few feet
before he
                goes
                        down

"just a rubber bullet   he'll be all right"

says a cop   who asks   "did you see the knife?"

and nobody speaks

but the man with the saxophone   blows

and the buses   get through

I lift my eyes   toward the purple night sky

I look at the stars   the stars look (shy) — not bright.
                                               dim, dark night

like little white boys   running away

with their knees pulled up   under their chins

and a saxophone sings   a lonely song

and a saxophone dreams   somewhere   to call home

and a saxophone screams   on granville street

after midnight jazz   along granville street

four years old

my mother brought home another bad actor from the bar
but this guy was different
he was dangerous
I could sense it
she just wanted some laughs and somebody to drink with
he had one thing in mind
he grabbed her
tore open her blouse
she yelled
he pressed against her
grinning

I went after him
tried to pull him off her
he swore
threw me across the room
she was really scared
begging him to stop

I ran at him again
he hit me hard
threw me into the wall
she screamed at me to stay there
she stopped struggling
he pushed her down on the couch
spread her legs
undid his pants

I squeezed my eyes shut
shoved my hands against my ears
I wanted to tear myself to pieces
I could still hear her sobbing
I could still hear him panting and grunting
I didn't want to feel what I was feeling
it was too much

and that was how evil entered me
like a knife
I vowed I would never again be vulnerable
to another human being

steele

no heat
no electricity
no bottles to bleed
nothing in the refrigerator
but empty pots and pans
no tobacco
not a cent

everybody else
anywhere else

except for me and steele
sitting in his room
in our low-down rooming-house

ice islands were becoming ice continents
on the inside of the window

and steele
with his silver hair and ragged red sweater
was still staring at the floor
hunched on the edge of his bed
his face in his hands

I thought of that statue
"the thinker"
and laughed and said
"it's never got down this far before
we ain't even got half a lousy match"

in the months I'd known him
I'd never seen steele
so paralyzed
by a situation

so I just sat there

cold wind rattling the walls

our last candle stub
flickering
faster
and faster

abruptly steele stood up
and said
"let's go!"

I was shocked
steele hated leaving his room
during the best of times

we stumbled down dark alleys
crossed side streets
plowed through fields of snow and frozen bricks
skidded through playgrounds covered with ice
and ran through backyards
where dogs barked

steele never said where we were going
he didn't say a word

we emerged onto well-lit streets
where people with money
were moving between
shops and movies and restaurants and taverns

steele was ahead of me
passing a fashionably-dressed young couple

when I got to them I said
"excuse me"
and wrenched a death-rattle cough through my lungs
I gagged on it

they were staring at me

I looked for steele
and yelled the first thing
that came into my head
"hey dad! wait up will ya?"

"I'm sorry for bothering you" I told them
"but my father hasn't eaten in a couple of days
he's getting sick
and I was wondering if you could spare
a nickel or a dime
so we could get some soup or a sandwich?"

I don't know if they heard a word I said
transfixed as they were
by steele
walking slowly towards us
glaring at me

steele removed his hat
pulled a handkerchief
wiped his brow
looked at me
with a face turned very grey and weary
sighed and said
"son

how many times have I told you
not to go up to people on the street
and ask them for money?"

though he never once looked at them
the two young people never took their eyes
off steele
replacing his hat
walking away hunched over
shaking his head sadly

I don't know how many people laughed at us
or how many believed us
but when I followed steele
into the wine store just before closing
quarters and dimes and nickels
were literally
spilling out of my pockets

four bottles of wine
tobacco
rolling papers
matches
shit paper
candles

then steele vanished

he had the bags in his arms
we were back on the street
and he disappeared around a corner

I climbed into a taxi
and rode back to the darkened rooming-house

I walked up the stairs
through the hallway
towards the glow
coming from steele's room

he had a glass of wine
already poured for me

I sat down in his battered armchair
and stared at him

finally
steele looked up

he grinned

and said
"that's not something
you can do everyday
you know?"

the point

when they give acting awards
they ought to have a special category
for drug addicts trying to score shots
in hospital emergency wards

afterwards
the doctor asked me how I felt
I told him I was still in pain
the doctor looked bewildered and said
"but we gave you the same amount of demerol
we give a broken leg"
"I don't know" I said "but it's not enough"

but this is the point I'd reached
this is how huge my habit
I had to get the drugs
I had to

I decided to go out on the streets at night
with a hammer concealed in my clothing
and search for someone
who looked vulnerable
and like they might have
a couple of bucks

I was going to
sneak up quietly behind them
whack them over the head
and take their money
'you might kill or maim somebody'
said a voice in my head

but I had to get some money
I had to

and it was just at this moment
hefting the hammer in my hand
sweating and shaking
I saw a pitch-black hole
open in front of me
like one of those black holes in space
that grabs all the light near it
sucks the light into its hole
and crushes it

and so I suppose I made a choice
not to
but it was this vision
more formidable than the furies of my addiction
the care from another human being
a friend I could not
drive away
that started me
towards a new life

I had a lot going for me
but if I hadn't
like so many addicts I have known
don't
it might have been your life
your hopes
your dreams
in the way
of the hammer
of my desperation

gentrification

"gentrification: to convert an aging area in the city into a more affluent middle-class neighbourhood, resulting in increased property values and in displacement of the poor"
—WEBSTER'S NEW WORLD DICTIONARY

"gentrification . . . a revengeful and reactionary viciousness against various populations accused of 'stealing' the city from the white upper classes"
—NEIL SMITH, THE NEW URBAN FRONTIER

1

    drunk & crazy I dance & chant & plead through a photograph of my father for him to be relieved of the consequences of his suicide & cease plaguing me & marie's down in bed sick as hell & ricky hood's hanging out the window serenading street hookers with maritime outlaw ballads & I open a newspaper to the sacred numbers "7 new buildings going up 4 the fashion industry 3 for the computer industry" & last august marie & I were evicted because of renovations from an apartment we'd lived in for 3 years & walked back & forth across the city through a record heatwave sweating & swearing & hungry & desperate to find something besides $450-a-month rooms where psycho coconuts crash through the doors & marie was bitten in the ass by a dog she startled behind one of the dumps we looked at & whipped-to-shit I went to a doctor who gave me anti-depression pills which launched me into a homicidal-paranoid delirium "look at that guy mowing his lawn" I said to marie "I think he's trying to kill me but I'm gonna get him first" & when we finally rent a rare vacant room at the hotel isabella we're so relieved to be off the street we don't at first notice the evidence of renovation all around us but the 2 blue harmonica boxes I place on the table in our tiny room do look like little coffins ready to bury the reduced lives we lead & now fire alarms shriek in the hallway & the lights have blacked-out but no one seems to know why

2

ricky hood from next door's pounding on our door he's on parole & wine & valium & playing an unplugged electric guitar & singing "ufos over houston!" the rats are clawing wailing & hurling themselves against the flimsy barricades I built to protect a last loaf of stale bread & fire engines scream through the black & yellow window the radio's reporting annual family holiday massacres & bottle-bombs thrown from the high-rise pressure cooker across sherbourne street explode on the sidewalk & smash sunroofs out of parked cars & young wingnuts are down on the block wrecking storefronts fighting police & a raggedy bum bellows "why light up city hall? blow it up!" & new year's day talks in its sleep complaining to no avail the ultraviolet blues of unbeaten emergencies in our home in hell in room 41 of a downtown misfits' hotel under renovation-siege the new owner like a toxic fire starting in the basement panicking every living thing in painting the walls white & pink & I'm turning over a dead leaf with a glass of gut-burning tap water a handful of codeine & last night's butts for breakfast & the top floor phantom's singing down the stairwell "losers make their own way!" & marie & I struggle through a long line for food we can't use without machinery we don't have & in front of us a friendly filthy young man wearing a thick bandage over a bad burn "passed out" he said "against a radiator" & shoved up his shirt to reveal old wounds burned black & purple to the bone & laughed & said "I'm into pain!" & our foodbank-footsteps in the snow are melting through roses fading on the carpet

3

smoke a cigarette & stare at the high-rise crushing my eyes
stare into someone's room into their eyes staring back at me it's
horrible & from the street a voice explodes "I don't give a damn!"
& I scream "I can't stop drinking!" & marie screams "you don't
want to!" & throws the i ching & I read edgar poe's vision of a time
before "the demon of the engine" when only "the red man trod"
& now there are notices of lock changes & rent-in-advance & evic-
tions for dirty bathrooms & a drunken brawl in the bar downstairs
& tension between marie & I like magritte's painting of this giant
rock filling a small room & a hyacinth blooms on our frozen win-
dowsill & some spontaneous hooker chorus sings from the side-
walk "it's a good night for a hold-up!" poe wrote "I fled in vain" &
outlaws & outcasts revolve through our door a dozen times a day
& it gets so you fart you violate somebody's space you belch &
that's an accusation & you're finally condemned for being yourself
on purpose with no maps guides or gyroscopes for the situation
like the hotel dope dealer busting dope smokers smoking dope
he's sold them trying to keep his desk clerk job for the new boss
who bought this hotel he said "to get rich and have fun!" & the la-
bel tells me to "take one sedative at bedtime" & I take 5 to stay
awake & in her terrible sleep marie says one word "angels"

4

john throws his mop & bucket at his woman & charlie
screams & slams the door & walks out on his girlfriend & lucy
down the hall goes after her man with a knife & joe beats joyce
pretty badly after she breaks a bottle over his head & dust clouds
& paint fumes scorch the air & our instincts are twisted like scorpi-
ons who sting themselves & each other panicked by a burning
stick shoved into their nest & another notice bans all pets except I
guess for rats & roaches & "shitpants" the old guy in the bar says
"change is good it weeds out the undesirables" not realizing he's

the next undesirable to be uprooted overnight & the new boss gives tours to prospective clientele & complains to them about the "deadbeats and dopers and welfare bums" making his renovations difficult & outside on the street a sign on the side of a taxicab proclaims "the intelligence of money"

5

I turn on the radio & reola jackson from cummins prison sings "I been hurt, same as you" & I use the phone & a woman tells me "I am not a branch I'm an information centre" & I tell her "I thought you were a human being" but all that's changed & slams us into distant corners with our backs against the punched cracked walls & silence between us like thunder from the mouth of hell & after I drink up all our money I try to stab ron with a pair of scissors but marie shoves him out the door & blackens my eye with a right hook & ron runs down to the front desk screaming "there's two people trying to kill each other in room forty-one," but they tell him "you're drunk go away" so ron & I get drunker and blast the hotel with his electric keyboards & the harmonica I don't know how to play & when they bang on the door ron throws 2 glasses & an empty bottle at it & I stagger raving into the hallway where marie hauls me into our room & so we narrowly avoid eviction before we're scheduled to be evicted what a relief

6

marie refuses to go to the hospital with me & is too sick to go herself & it's the middle of the night & I'm in the middle of the street & it's the middle of winter & I can't take it anymore so I grab a bag & out the door feeling torn to pieces screaming at each other "bullshit!" "fuck you!" & I go to our friend heljo who was officially a "displaced person" during world war 2 & she translates a poem for me by juhan liiv an estonian poet who died in a madhouse

"our room has a black ceiling
it's black and smoky
there are cobwebs
there's soot
and so much
so much pain
o lord have mercy
our room has a black ceiling
and so does our time
which is twisting in chains
if only it could talk"

I walk back & say the poem to marie who cries & cries & I don't know what to do but the construction workers tell loud racist jokes & the new owner brags about "a dress code . . . big changes . . . I want to sell sex" & residents like jerry & lois who never drank before the renovations are getting drunk everyday now & a mouse races across the carpet & cold wind & rain rip at the window & finally I bring cold rags to reduce marie's temperature & I bring her soup & I pound on my head with my fists & I sit on the toilet & push a knife point into my belly & I shake & hyperventilate & smell gas fumes leaking into the air & I hear laughter from somewhere & a junkie bangs on the door & nods off on the floor & somebody else needs something else & the hard-to-love are dealt down & dirty & go down the drain with so many of us insisting what is happening here will never happen not here 'not to me I've been here too long' never change an old blues hotel into an upscale fern-dripping sports bar & tourist accommodation but early this dark morning very early this very dark morning I pick a gold coin out of a snowbank what do you know?

7

10 years since we ran from the isabella all the way to vancouver & I've been flown back to speak at a theological conference on "driving god out matthew 25 and the homeless" &

though marie & I have now taken separate paths she's become a chaplain & abides with those dying of aids or other afflictions & becomes for them & their relatives & lovers & friends a bridge between life & death & became in vancouver a bridge from death to new life for me & I remember this native guy in the bar at the isabella telling a man bugging marie to "leave her alone she's a shaman" marie's a cherokee from the hills of oklahoma & has visceral memories of the "trail of tears" that genocidal displacement of cherokees from the carolinas & finally marie told me about that night she really was dying of pneumonia & I was drunk & chanting & dancing & said her spirit departed her body & soared into a sky of light where she encountered my father's darkness & guided him across a threshold before returning from what a doctor told marie was a "near death" experience but all I know that since that scary night in room 41 I haven't sensed my father's frantic presence pressuring me & approaching the isabella I expect to see an upscale enterprise has erased the old hotel & displaced all the misfit inhabitants & wonder what new monstrosity of redevelopment looms amid toronto's global city agenda driving people into every doorway along bloor street after dark but astonishment shoots through me like a jump blues tune as one of the least of us a raggedy old man goes through the isabella's front door with a key in his hand & I look above at the streaked & smudged & smeared sign inscribed with a single beautiful word ROOMS

street sermon

AFTER HEARING ONE TOO MANY PREACHERS HARANGUING ABOUT HELL-
FIRE ON GRANVILLE STREET.

brothers and sisters   fellow low-life   listen   we are in luck   one
guy at least   came just for us   a tremendous low-life   jesus   he
didn't come down here   to this blood-stew   for no limousine
riders   no bible thumpers   no hotshot angle-shooters   no
came down here   I believe it's the truth   for me and you   I
mean   junkies   winos   hookers   cripples   crazies   thieves
welfare bums   and homeless freaks   lowest of the low   least of
all

do your parents hate you?   your teachers hate you?   po-lice
hate you?   your friends hate you?   you hate you?   you're
really in luck   everybody hated jesus too   you got nowhere to
live?   nowhere to go?   nowhere to hang your hat?   jesus said
to a cat   'even the foxes of the field   and the birds of the air
got somewhere   to lay their weary ass down   but not me   oh
no'

do people scorn you?   put you down?   tell stories about what
a problem you are?   a judge told me   I was of no use to society
the president of a university   told me I was trash and obscene
my own mother   god bless her   told me I was the world's
biggest asshole   but all that   just makes me eligible   to hook
up with jesus   who got nailed up   bleeding   sweating   balls-
naked   to a wooden cross   to take all that bad bullshit   off my
back

jesus tells you   not to hate your own self   which is easy to do
out here   running around like a fool   but just ask jesus   he'll

help you with that   'love yourself' he says   'so you can love
somebody as   unloved   and unlovable   as you been'

I mean   jesus didn't come all this way   go through all that
trouble   to send you and me to hell   no   maybe these other
soft successful types   I don't know   but not you and me   bona
fide losers   you and I know   this world   is all the hell   we're
going to see   jesus came to cool us out   from this hell   right
here   right now   for real   with love   not handcuffs   editorials
or plastic gloves

do you slash up?   overdose?   drink lysol?   stick rigs in your
arms?   or pull a knife on somebody else?   well   jesus is just for
you   he was the world's   all-time   biggest   loser   the straight
people   the priests   and judges   hated him   because   he said
low-life scum   would get to heaven   before they did

and at the end   when jesus needed his friends   they all took off
on him   except for a hooker   named magdalene   but all his
close friends   split   said 'no way I don't know him' except for
his friend judas   who turned jesus in   to crimestoppers   his
friends made him   take the rap   all alone   you know how that
feels   and jesus   kept his mouth shut   when pontius pilate
the chief of police   wanted jesus to cop-out   with a plea

so if you feel misunderstood   nobody know how you feel   or
what you talking about   that's jesus too   he know about you
he been through it   and don't you allow these   puffed-up
self-righteous chumps   sell you no   goody-goody jesus   hell
no   jesus got pissed-off plenty times

and when jesus was   wandering around   no bus fare   all his
buddies kept saying   'what should we do?   what should we
do?   we're scared'   jesus told them   'lay down your life for

your friends   and if   your enemy   rip off your coat   give him
your shoes too   give up this   money-grubbing   power-tripping
fantasy-acting   ego bullshit   give it up   and you won't be
scared no more'

but jesus got   hung up   between two thieves   just another
criminal   and everybody thought so little   of jesus   was down
on him   so bad   they let   a mad terrorist bomber   go free
instead of him   but jesus told that thief   hanging on the cross
next door   like he telling you and me   'right now today   this
very hour man   I take you with me   to paradise'   jesus told a
death-row thief   he was going to take him   to paradise

jesus didn't tell   a stockbroker   didn't tell   a rock promoter
he told   the brokers and promoters   'you can't get to paradise
the way you going'   a young banker   came up to jesus   said
'I dig your rap   what I gotta do?'   and jesus told him   'give it
up brother'   said   'give all your money to the poor   the punks
the drunks   the bums   give it up'   and that banker   did to
jesus   what most people   do to you   when you got   your
hand out   he just walked away   'anything but my sports car'

even in his own hometown   they called jesus   a crazy bugger
I been called crazy   lots of times   in my hometown   locked up
in the nuthouse to prove it   and jesus   his neighbours told him
'we know you boy   don't go pullin   none of them miracles
around here'   and tried   to grab him   but he ran fast   damn
but you know   what that's like

and if you think   you got trouble   just keeping your name
straight   jesus   confused many fools   with that   'are you god
or what?'   they were always asking him   he said 'who do you
say that I am?'   a smart-ass   jesus was always being told   'you
can't do that   it's against the rules   it's against the law'   but
jesus talking about   the spirit   body and soul   the whole deal

42

real   real life   not just   bingo   lotteries   and videos

and jesus believed   in having a good time   told those tight-ass
bastards   his kingdom   was like a wedding reception   and first
thing jesus did   was turn water into wine   so they wouldn't run
out   and the authorities   called him   a drunkard   but jesus
kept saying   'help each other   love each other   no matter
what   it's the only thing   you can count on'

so   fellow low-life   just know   jesus loves you   if nobody else
does   I know he loves me   especially when I don't   love myself
or anybody else   it's hard to believe in love   in this cruel city   in
this   nightmare time   that everybody else pretends   is just fine
but remember   no matter what kind   of nasty shit you pull
jesus loves you   in fact   you can't make jesus   not love you

but when you been   kicked around   since you were born   love
is like an insult   'oh we love you so much   we want to hurt you
some more'   but not with jesus   when you suffering   real bad
just reach a hand   out of your   heart   and he'll help you make
it   jesus has already helped you make it   you just didn't know it

and the gospel tell you   the gospel just   the highlights of a
low-life   jesus believed   in the devil too   the devil that runs
around   in him   and her   and me   and you   and all over
everyplace else seems like   jesus knew the devil personally but
jesus didn't   go on and on   about some   therapy-self-help-
social worker-shrink-headed-victim-disease-shit   jesus knew we
couldn't be   this crazy   this miserable   this goddamned
mean and vicious   without a lot of help   from the devil   so
jesus   spooked the devil   right out of people   jesus knows
we're weak   and easily possessed   by all the crap   in this world
jesus   knows all this stuff

so the devil   came to see jesus   one on one   when jesus was

strung-out   from not eating   and hanging out   in the desert
near kamloops   and the devil said   to jesus   'if you such a
bigshot   turn this stone   into a whopper with cheese   and
feed your raggedy self'   and jesus said   'forget you   I'd rather
be   hungry   than do   what you tell me to do'   did you ever
do that?   refuse   and have people say   'you don't know
what's good for you?'

then the devil   said to jesus   'look here   I show you   all the
beer   cars   clothes   dope   power   sex   in the whole world
I'll give you all that   just say you're mine'   but jesus   could not
be bought   and the devil   kept working on him   the devil said
'okay   you so stupid   jump off this building   and see if your
big daddy save you   like you always talking about   jesus just
laughed   he knew better

I haven't always known better though   those deals   the devil
offered jesus   sound pretty good   to me   but I have been
mostly messed up   in my life   so I ain't the best expert   on my
own life   I do need help   so   all you   nuts   junkies   freaks
jesus is always   by your side   like a kind of   no bullshit   truth-
talking guide   always with you   but not   so close by   he'll get
on your nerves

I mean a lot of times you think   he's not there at all   cause he
ain't doing   what you think   he ought to be   doing for you
but he's there   knowing what you need   better than you do
knowing you   better than you do   just like   the devil do

but that's good   because everything   I know how to do   and
everything   you know how to do   has got us both   right here
probably broke   maybe on dope   no real hope   listening to a
lunatic like me   because neither of us   has figured out anything
better to do   with the   mountain-moving love   jesus   has
made us   all   to be

the truth of community

all day long
the horrible august sun
set them on fire
and machine guns
and attack dogs
and barbed-wire fences wired with electricity
where teenaged boys threw themselves
to escape
from auschwitz

a prisoner fled the camp
or so the nazis said
and lined the 600 men of barrack 14 into rows

the men were forbidden to speak
sit down
or take one step out of line
under penalty of immediate execution

all day long

until assistant camp commandant fritsch arrived
and announced that since
the escaped prisoner had not been found
10 of the men standing there would die

and fritsch began to walk the rows
examining the prisoners
selecting which of them would be
stripped naked
locked in a cellar half-buried in the earth
and kept there
until they starved to death

one of the condemned men
a young polish soldier
francis gajownicek
fell to his knees and cried out
that he had a young wife
and small children
and wanted to live

fritsch ordered the man to the starvation cell

but then
something extraordinary occurred
something unheard of in auschwitz

a man stepped forward out of the rows
and began to speak

fritsch commanded the man to get back into line
"have you gone mad?" fritsch shouted at him

but the prisoner calmly replied
that he wished to take
francis gajownicek's place

the man explained that since he himself
was old and ill
the nazis could get more work
from a younger man

and assistant camp commandant fritsch
according to witnesses
fell silent
and appeared stunned

the august sun burned the air
and auschwitz fell silent

fritsch pondered
then
astonishingly
rescinded his own order
and granted the prisoner's request

and so maximillian kolbe joined the other 9 men
stripped of their clothes
and interred in their tomb

kolbe's own hard-won community of franciscans
who had housed refugees
fed the poor
repaired the machinery of peasant farmers
and dispensed medicine to any who were in need
had been destroyed
his brothers murdered or sent to exile
and kolbe incarcerated in auschwitz

first the brain dehydrates
and hallucinates
but kolbe remained lucid
and comforted the others
they sang canticles of love
in a death cell
in auschwitz

and on the 14th day
when nazis entered the cell
to remove the bodies
maximillian kolbe
still alive

had to be killed
with an injection of phenic acid

kolbe
who created community even in auschwitz

kolbe
who lived community while naked and starving to death

kolbe
who sang community into a situation without hope

kolbe
who demonstrated that community cannot be destroyed
though buildings are demolished
though people are scattered and lives shattered

kolbe
who taught that community cannot be extinguished
as long as a single human being
steps forward
out of line
and speaks out
for the sake of another's life

kolbe

black on grey

FOR DONALD BOND

"poor soul"
the receptionist says
when I ask for you
steam & clouds make shadows in this still &
sterile room & you don't recognize an old
friend as I call your name & your eyes begin
closing so I shout & my voice feels evil & a
gasp from plastic tubing startles me
swollen & scarred
a hand floats
toward nothing
your legs useless beneath a white sheet your
chest shrinking my fingers tremble over your
hot pale forehead afraid of sinking them into
your brain's
vulnerable
lightning
saved an old man from a mugging but minutes
later the avenging thief returned for you &
crushed your skull with a wooden club silencing
your wild laughter & huge indignations & now
your eyes open & the right one moves not the one
blinded red & raw in the car crash that years
ago started it all downhill for an "adonis" with
a woman you loved & a job you wanted not scar
tissue growing over steel plates making the
thought of a drink an endless drunk you're
only 40 years old & your shaved head sprouts
tiny hairs like splinters driven in instead of
the black blaze of curls you wore with pride

49

                    searching for life
                    I see
                    a machine
breathing you & a machine tracing heartbeat in
measurable waves & lines & dots like your eye
traces me traces nothing ice cubes melting
shift where a suction tray is constructed
causing explosion in this steam-silent room
your blistered lips collapse together writhe
once in a while & I hear distant intercom
muzak subdued laughter of nurses & suddenly I
panic & wipe your sweat from my fingertips
afraid of you whom I've embraced many times
                    disoriented
                    shadows
                        tear the room apart
a black glance reflects on grey television
glass & I have hoped as all who come to see
you say they do that one of us–the lucky
one–will bring you back because our lives
are torment & we want to mean something
vital & you ridicule our fantasies more than
any painted corpse
                    helpless
                    I want
                    to kill you
I retch get angry & making my face a mask
walk into the hallway where a nurse notices
the room I leave & when our eyes lock our
embarrassment is horrifying the sky outside's
roaring blue wind
                    bright autumn sun
                    a leaf falls
                    I burst into tears
& want to say it's for you alone I feel deep

sadness but these tears belong to me who wants
to call 'liars' the doctors who say "vegetable" &
I want to deny that anyone who speaks as you
have of the strong spirit love is & of a yearning
to make well that which is ill can ever be
degraded like this though some people claim
you brought it on yourself & others implicate
survivors who failed you but we only know you
spent your last days laughing complaining &
sharing what you had drinking cheap wine &
sleeping in abandoned automobiles or on the
river bank & eating from garbage cans
       walking
       shoeless
       banned from agencies
becoming one less human to threaten anyone's
holy resumé "you're not going to fuck up my
referrals!" a social worker explained kicking
you out of a detox for the last time into the
street where as you often said:
       "you can't
       wear out
       the sidewalks"

street poem

stand/lean against a building
on west 8th street
in greenwich village
waitin for bill to show up
gonna get high on smack I'd scored earlier
go to a movie
I'm standin there
tourists surgin past
these two young people come right up to me
boy and girl both blonde and blazing blue eyes
freshfaced earnest evangelistic semi-delirious expressions
"do you believe in jesus?"
oh no I groan but feelin good
lookin forward to hangin out with bill
refined opium poppy already bloomin inside me

bill and I share an apartment
on carmine street
couple of blocks away
this one room place
4 adults
2 children
17 cats
a million cockroaches
a turtle in the bathtub
petey the big dog on a chain in the kitchen area
and a falcon in a large cage
bill's bird
glares ferociously
sometimes bill lets it out
swoops and flaps back and forth a few times
then looks to land on somebody's arm

not mine
not after the first time
falcon not trying to hurt anybody
but it's a big-ass bird of prey
very sharp talons
if it lands on your arm
you'll bleed

so these 2 born again fervent nutty kids
are givin it to me
bout jesus
I don't give a shit
killin time
then WHAM
3 monster-size new york city beat cops
bull me into a hallway behind me
one of them blocks the door to the street
they go through my pockets
shootin questions

are you buyin or sellin?
what're you talkin about? I say
you mean you don't have any drugs?
no I tell the cop I don't use em
then what's this? he says
pullin a pill bottle full of pot
out of my coat pocket
oh I said I didn't think you meant grass
when you were askin did I have drugs
is this methadone? the other cop asks
holdin a pint of unopened gin
I had in my back pocket
yeah I say they're sellin methadone
in the liquor store now
the cop waves a small wad of money in front of me

where'd you get this?
man I say
and I am really indignant
self-righteous and aggrieved
for one of the few times
I can say it for real
in my life
man I say to the cop
I
gotta
job
I just got off work
I was paid today
look here I say
I whip out my wallet
the heroin's tucked away in it
I remove my fleet messenger service identity card
say look right here
the doorway blocker cop sticks his head in and says
what'd you find on him?
the other cop holds up the pill bottle
oh well the doorway cop says give it back to him
so the cop does
hands me the pill bottle
and says don't ever lie to us
when we ask if you got drugs
no I won't I tell him
and be cool he says but get high somewhere else
okay man don't worry bout me
he's in the doorway
he turns around and looks at me and says
when was the last time you ate?
askin like I wasn't takin care of myself or somethin
I had a slice of pizza a hour ago I tell him
whinin like I'm bein police brutalized
and the cops go down the street

but the 2 newly hatched christian inquisitors
are still standin right there
wide-eyed
lookin at me
what happened? the boy asks
it's all your fault I tell him
get the fuck away from me
what'd we do? asks the girl
she looks crestfallen
a nice word and good place to get to use it
crestfallen
I say I mean it get away from me
the cops think I'm tryin to sell you drugs
you got me in trouble
their jaws drop so far down
that big-ass bird of bill's could build a nest in there
but they're still standin right in front of me
I say jesus woulda never treat somebody like this
and that's it
they walk slowly away
their heads hangin
bill comes up
fuck's goin on? he says
these kids are tryin to buy drugs offa me I tell him
fuck them bill says
let's go to the movie

jackson avenue and east hastings

little bird barely feathered
fallen from your nest prematurely
flexing wings too weak to lift you
from this hard luck street corner
of heavy traffic and hungry predators
how long will you survive little bird?
will the miracle within your tiny wings
save you in time?

or the little girl barely dressed
across the street on her own dangerous corner
waving thin and frail arms
attracting like your wings
not flight but the attention
of killers?

I was in jail

I was in jail, some suburb of Los Angeles. A tail light had burned out. A cop stopped the car I was riding in and smelled marijuana. He found a few joints in my pocket and took me to the police station where I was locked in a holding tank.

The tank's floor was hard rubber with a hole in the middle and a large plexi-glass window spread all the way across the front.

After awhile, a young guy was put in there with me. He was clean-cut with short hair, and well-dressed. He sat down with his back against the wall and stared at a spot in front of him. He never spoke a word. He never looked around, not even when cops came to the front of the tank—

cops—one after another—or bringing cops from somewhere else—to show off—the monster.

"There he is!" they sneered. "That's him!" they said with contempt, glaring at the young guy, who looked to me like he thought his life was over. He'd been drunk earlier, but appeared stone cold sober now. Drunk and driving fast. Then, how does it happen?

I've been so drunk I've driven right over a stop sign. I've driven right through a fire hydrant. I've driven so drunk I passed out at the wheel. But I never did what this young guy did.

He crossed a centre line, head-on into another. A terrible crash. The young man didn't have a scratch. But the old man driving the other car was killed, and so was his infant granddaughter riding next to him.

I watched cops come to the front of the tank until my 4 hours of waiting for bail was up, and they moved me to a cell-block in back.

Cops kept saying, "That's the one! That's him right there!" Pointing at the young guy like they were aiming a loaded crucifix at the devil himself.

And I'd look over at him. I'd look at the killer, sitting so still, looking like his own life was over. He didn't have a scratch on his skin.

In the years since then I've wondered, from time to time, whatever became of him?

Did he allow the wound ripped in his soul to heal? Or did he fasten onto it and let it grow until it devoured him?

And the little girl—who remembers her?

beyond a reasonable doubt

the very air had become yellow sheets of flame

I went into a bar
early in the morning
only a couple guys in there
besides the bartender

I was oh so friendly
oh so gregarious
I shot a game of eight-ball with one guy
sat next to another guy
cracked jokes
and asked him questions

I ingratiated myself so well
the guy bought me several drinks
and showed me a gun he had with him

and just when he thought
he could relax with me
just when he believed
we were on the same wave-length
and becoming fast friends
I insulted the guy

he wasn't sure he heard me right
he let it go

I insulted him again
I knew him well enough by then
to make it personal

at first he was hurt
he'd trusted me
he thought he liked me
he thought he knew me
he thought I liked his company

but then he got angry
and was right where I'd been leading him

I got off my bar stool
walked a few feet to the front door
turned around
and insulted the guy once more
as deeply as I could

he jumped from his stool
pulled out the gun
aimed it right at me

I opened my stance
to give him a wide-open shot
at my heart

I said to him
"come on . . . shoot . . .
what are you . . . a coward?"

I looked in his eyes
he looked in mine
horror gripped his

he dropped the gun

I laughed at him

I walked outside
and thrilled
imagining his conversation
with the police
if he'd killed me—

a detective saying to him
"let me get this straight . . . this guy was leaving the bar . . . he
was unarmed . . . he wasn't threatening you in any way . . . he
said something you didn't like . . . and you got off your stool . . .
took out the gun . . . and shot him dead . . . is that right?"

the real story
of what goes on between human beings
never comes out in court
or in the newspapers

and only rarely
in the understanding
of those involved

the very air becomes yellow sheets of flame

a vital profession

BLOOD PLASMA CONTAINS PROTEIN, WHICH IS THE PRIMARY
SUBSTANCE IN ALL LIVING MATTER.

on lower monroe street
tarnished bronze balls of a pawn shop
huddle in a cold grey wind

the restaurant and saloon supply
              the labour pool
              and brenda's body shop
collide with sandblasted brick office buildings

ragged men on the corner
try to work up the price
of a warm white port breeze

traffic
coming from the west
from suburbs
slashes past them

I walk in
go up to the desk
and sign my name under
RETURNING DONORS

a tall slender black woman
in a white uniform
is sweeping an old bum out the door:

"you know you can't donate when you been drinkin!"

he's heard it before but still can't believe it
and his slow wide grin
is torn right off his face
by the rush hour wind on monroe street

I sit down to wait
and a young black guy asks me if I got
a "j"

I tell him I haven't
and then like an anguished wind blowing out of him
he raps a long solo:

"I been back only a week from the coast
man
out there it's cool
but I flipped out
17 days in a hospital
thinkin I was jesus christ
I'm only 23

"but out there
del rey
venice
santa monica
charlie manson and the family
well
I was with the family
and this white dude
he got his own business goin
you know he was cool
he gave me a job but I fucked it up
usin drugs
and didn't handle it like a man

"I was losin it when I left here
it wasn't the drugs
I was usin more stuff here than I was out there
but I'm a family man
got 2 little babies
I did one in
the abortion thing
that was on my head
and here I am down here
and I want to go back out there

"my woman works
I'm livin with my people here
when she saves a couple grand
we'll go out there and buy a house
cause I'm a family man
and I got a trade out there
dry cleanin
this white dude started me
see these boots?
he did that
he's cool
but I fucked up

"and I don't take my pills
man
that zino is a nice high
but it weighs me down
I can't finish a sentence
and I like to talk to people
just go up to people
and talk
not like these people here
around here shit
they so cold
they don't want to talk

"out there there's no ghettos
I mean like these buildings here
all dark and empty
people livin upstairs
cramped in
people are friendly out there
but I didn't go to the valley
or watts

"but like
I'm physically disabled
because I'm physically disabled
thinkin I'm jesus christ
because I'm jesus christ
I should be able to get money for it
but the welfare people here
don't want to do nothin
for me

"I went to the labour pool
and they got nothin
and here I am doin this shit
this is awful
now they got women comin down here
my people wanted me to come back
after I got out the hospital out there
and now I'm here
doin this shit!"

somebody calls my name
and I weigh in

an attendant asks me if my answers are
NO
to all the questions

about whether or not I've had any
drugs
booze
or transfusions
in the last 24 hours
I say
YES

and sit down again to wait for the line-up

the young black guy has walked out

over loudspeakers
a radio station is pushing remedies:

"hey man!"

"yeah baby!"

"what's that you got in the paper sack?"

"ain't nothin man!"

"yeah it's a bottle of night train wine!
I can tell by the smoke of that locomotive
in your eyes!"

"yeah man but it's all mine!"

"oh come on man give me a taste!"

"okay man here!"

"ahhh yeaahh!"

"so get your night train wine
a velvet express
to pleasure!"
an attendant holds a stack of files
and reads off 8 names

8 of us line up and have our

                temperature taken
                blood pressure measured
                fingers pricked
                protein counted
and get handed 2 plastic bags
with our individual number pasted all over them

a skinny black man standing next to me says:

"I don't mind needles
but they use little knives here!"

the worst thing that could happen
and the first thing the doctor assures you
has never happened
is that you'll get the wrong bag of blood back—
instant shock

the doctor used to be
a top shrink
at the nuthouse
and hit the large cans of liquid drugs
first thing in the morning
until he got locked up

"it's very safe and harmless" he says
"nothing serious happens
we process 500 bags a week!"

one old guy is
waiting for the doctor to thump his chest
and the creases and furrows on his stained hat
continue down the stubble fields
of his face

he's peering at the information sheet
we have to complete once in a while
and says:

"occupation?
hell I'm a perfessional man!
that's what I tell em in court
everytime they ask if I'm employed
I say 'why yes
        I'm a perfessional plasma donor!' "

money

5 dollars the first visit and 10 the second
but it's got to be in the same 5-day work week
I've heard in columbus it's 8 and 12
and in st. louis it's 10 and 15
but today I hear it all:

"25 and 25 in philly!"

"must have a building big as the sports arena!"
I say to a small black man in the chair
across from me

"no man" he says
"more like a barber shop
nobody goes in philly
like the dude that runs this place

I can't figure
how he can go to sleep with hisself at night
I couldn't sleep with myself
this shit little bit of money
you know what they make off us?"

I shake my head

"I don't know how he lives with hisself!" he says

we're laid back in 48 plastic-covered
                    vinyl-cushioned armchairs
                    with kick-out footrests

and pump our blood through a tube
into a plastic bag
dangling
off a scale beside the chair
and when the bag's filled
the scale tips over
and an attendant takes it away

this is a large room with a long counter at one end
where blood is separated from protein
with whirling machines
and the blood returned to our veins

there's a toilet off the hallway
dark with blood-stained mirror
and slippery with pools of piss

an old man in the chair beside me
blood vessels exploded all over his face
and blood-shot eyes
is reading

a battered paperback copy
of the red badge of courage

and a young long-haired guy on the other side
is examining his bag
and says:
>   "I was sittin here one day watchin a guy pump
>   and nobody came to check his bag
>   he kept pumpin
>   and that bag split
>   man
>   the blood gushed all over the floor
>   it was somethin!"

there's a lump swelling in the hollow of my elbow
something's jammed
I yell for an attendant
she comes over and strips the tube
with blunt scissors
this usually means you have to get re-stuck
and I don't know anyone
who has ever gotten used to
>   the
>   long
>   thick
>   hollow
>   needle

but like everybody else
I try to act
as if it doesn't bother me

the attendant's twisting the needle
trying to get a flow going
my skin stretches and stretches—

the line clears

and we bullshit awhile
until the pale young woman a few chairs down
a smiling red-haired first-timer
goes under
her wide eyes fluttering closed

her husband's 6 chairs away
watching and squirming
because he's stuck and running
and can't do anything

the attendants and the doctor
pop amyl nitrate under her nose
lift her feet in the air
put a pyramid-shaped board beneath her legs
check her blood pressure

and she comes to

the cat from philly is sunk deep in his chair
he stares with contempt
shakes his head in disgust

the woman's husband yells:

"hey don't stick her again!"

but he's too late
they've got the needle in her other arm
and they're running her again

"oh she's okay now" an attendant tells her husband

and behind me somebody snarls:

"hey!
don't get near me you fuck!
what do you do for your money?
you fuck!"

a white guy's hooked in a chair
barking at a black dude
who's dancing around on elevator-heels
wearing a wide-brimmed hat
and joking with the attendants

the black dude snaps a punch
at the white guy
on his way out the door
and they promise to meet each other
later

a hillbilly near me
gets mad at an attendant
because she's taking her time
changing his bag
and that's a mistake
he'll wait that much longer

"that guy said he's gonna shoot me!"
the attendant said
"gonna fix me!
 I thought he meant with a gun!
 but he said he was gonna overdose me!
 with heroin!
 I told him not to waste it
 just
 give it to me!"

and all the attendants are laughing
at the hillbilly whose eyes are murdering them

the attendants have their favourites
and so do we
some attendants stick crude
and some stick clean
some take care of business
others wander and dream

I pump 2 bags out
and 2 more pour cold blood
back into my veins

only 4 hours for the 5 dollars today
and I am handed an Icebag
to reduce the swelling

I want to grab the money and get out quick
but I've jumped out of the chair too soon before
reached for my coat
and watched my blood leap
into the air

the hole the needle made finally closes
I go out front to collect
and a young white guy
                              with a shaved skull
                              and cobra tattoos
says to an old old black man:

"I just got out of the joint old man!
  14 months in mansfield!"

but the old man does a little step
away from the boy glaring
                        down
                        at
                        him

and says gently as he can:
                        "that's okay son"

outside a bitter wind still rips the street
   the traffic is heading west
      to the suburbs
         and we drift east
            across a dirty green river
               on a suspension bridge painted blue

terrorism

I was talking with a kid who told me
his grade school classmate
was killed
in the air india massacre
and his school
held a large memorial service
attended by
all the other children and parents
who prayed for the soul
of the murdered boy
and for themselves
who'd suffered such a deep loss

so I asked the kid what the boy was like?

"I don't know" he said
"nobody'd play with him
because he got bad grades
and his skin was brown"

we reserve the right

I was on a baseball team in southern missouri
I was 14 years old
I was from ohio and the other boys
came from all over north america
and we travelled to our games
in an old airport limousine
we played mostly in small towns
and one afternoon after a game
we stopped at a greasy spoon
I was the first one of us inside the place
with paul a kid from washington d.c.
paul was a nice friendly kid
and a damned good ballplayer
we sat down at the counter
and gave our order to this guy wearing an apron
the rest of the team had piled in by then
I was hungry
and waited for my food
looking around
talking to paul
then I noticed other orders being delivered
burgers fries shakes
placed in front of other kids
I got restless
I wondered what happened to paul's order and mine
I said "hey!"
to the guy moving around behind the counter
but I couldn't get his attention
and I got bugged
paul and I were the first ones to sit down
we were the first ones to order
I didn't know what was going on
but paul was sitting on his stool

all calm and cool
not looking around
not doing anything
but I could never get the attention
of the guy behind the counter
he never even looked at me
even when he was standing right in front of me
I watched the rest of the team finish eating
I watched them pay for their food
and then they went back outside
and got in the limousine
"damn!" I said to paul
then it dawned on me
paul took me by the arm
"come on man" he said "let it go"
he led me out the door
but in the parking lot I told the coach
we had to do something
"have everybody grab a baseball bat
and go back inside!"
I was furious
paul was still calm and cool
"forget it man" he said
and he climbed into the limousine
well if paul wasn't going to do anything
I had no reason to
I didn't understand paul's response then
but now I know
he would've paid a much heavier price
than the rest of us
for any trouble we caused
because it was paul's fault we didn't get served
paul was
after all
the only black kid
on the team

global chant

in the regent park housing project
half a dozen black women
are lined up on the sidewalk
across the street
from the police division

little kids
and babies in strollers
are licking popsicles
and watching
intently and quietly
their mothers chanting
at white cops looking out the windows at them

chanting:

"die you cocksuckers!
we're gonna beat you to death!
fuckin   cops   die!"

a constable comes out the door
and the women
chant:

"yeah go 'head!
come over here!
we're gonna beat you to death!"

a cruiser drives slowly past them
the women move towards it

"and fuck you too!"

they chant

"fuckin   cops   die!"

the passion of the downtown eastside

after the board of directors meeting at the carnegie community centre I walk outside the theatre where the meeting was held to the balcony overlooking an alley to smoke a cigarette

in the alley I see a man methodically going through the trash in an overflowing dumpster and he reminds me of men I've seen panning for gold in rock creek

I see empty syringe packages floating or sunken in dark and dirty pools of water and I see a pink blouse in a heap and drug addicts scurrying to fix and I hear shouts and screams and curses and sirens blaring

and I see a woman wearing a sleeveless white blouse with large purple polka dots and a short white skirt with blue stripes

she's barefoot and has a multitude of bruises up and down her legs and black needle marks on the backs of her knees like a swarm of ants feasting on something sweet

and there are needle tracks on her arms and on her jugular vein and she has open sores and cuts and scratches and a white gauze bandage around one wrist the bandaging of a kind I've known to cover stitched and slashed wrists for even china white can't quiet the flashbacks ignited from a childhood of rape and beatings and abandonment so common down here

and then
this woman
grips a shopping cart for balance
and dances

her body

twists   bends   writhes
crouches and rises
as though thrust by a demon
into grotesque positions

the man sifts through trash
drug addicts walk past
with scarcely a glance
at this woman performing
a drug-driven dance
frequently seen
on the 100 block
of east hastings street

"the dance of the damned"
I say to a friend standing next to me
he grunts in acknowledgment

"should take them all out to the country"
he says
"and make them clean up
and if they want to leave
they'll have to walk a long way"

I don't tell him about junkies I've known
who have walked back down here
all the way from abbotsford
after leaving a treatment centre

my friend shakes his head in disgust
and departs
and still she dances
in an alley like a cesspool at the bottom of hell

but then she
grasps a slender piece of wood
from the shopping cart
snaps it
and dances a few feet to a wooden hydro pole

she lifts the object she made
above her head

she stands on one leg
and reaches to place it
between the metal sheath around the pole
and the wood

it's a cross

a wooden cross

her action is the culmination
of her dance
she spins away from the pole
bends over as though bowing down
takes 3 quick little steps
and is gone

sirens   screams   curses   shouts

she danced the passion
she raised a cross
here
for me
because I too have used drugs and spilled my blood
in this forsaken alley

in this dirty alley

she made a cross
from a useless piece of wood
a piece of wood the builders rejected

she made a cross
here
for the one
who stands most of all with the damned
the one whose cross
is the only sense
of her life and mine

in this abominable alley
she planted the cross
the cross cast out by churches of wealth and success
the cross denied in society
by the powers of success and wealth

she placed the truth
exactly where it belongs
exactly here
she made a place for him
perhaps the only place left for him
though he would be in every place

and she
knows where christ is
this woman
of all people
is the one chosen
to make this known
today

before my friend left he expressed
sentiments similar to those said about

the one who died on the cross–

"why doesn't somebody clean up this alley?"

my friend has only to wait a short time
for powers are aligning to do so
the same powers driving jesus away
because here is a cross
that cancels distinctions

between she who dances in an alley
and the daughters of power on robson street
who buy thin gold crosses
to hang around flawless necks
and unmarked skin

but here
in this alley
the cross is dangerous
this cross asks
"why have you forsaken me?"

here
in this alley
the cast-out christ asks
"why have you forsaken me?"
the one cursed by the world
the object of clean-up campaigns
the immoral one asks
god asks
"why have you forsaken me?"

it is an astonishment
and an amazement

this blessing
given here
in the most disgusting
location in the city

but what words should I then use
to describe
the stock exchange on granville street?

the stock exchange where there is no cross
no truth
no blessing

the stock exchange which tries
with other powers of lies and greed
to drive god
drive christ
drive her and me
from this city

except here
in this alley made holy
here
in this alley
one place at least
made holy

and you
who danced the passion of the downtown eastside
in faithfulness
surpassing understanding
may the peace of our lord jesus christ
be with you
always

hastings park haiku

HASTINGS PARK IS A THOROUGHBRED HORSE RACING TRACK IN EAST
VANCOUVER.

THE "RACING FORM HAIKU" ARE 'FOUND' HAIKU TAKEN FROM "PAST
PERFORMANCES" REPORTS ON INDIVIDUAL HORSES PRINTED IN THE
DAILY RACING FORM.

I'm at home here
everywhere I turn
a loser

racing form haiku:

"squeezed early
stumbled
lost all chance"

we search
past performances
for a safe bet now

3 minutes to post time
we rush the betting windows
mountains sit in silence

our horse leads
our horse
fades

Irony & tone.

racing form haiku:

"trapped
  most
  of the trip"

crows
on the finish line
eat horseshit

glassed in
against the track and the trash
the clubhouse patrons
        り てうたい？

beneath the whip
"sailaway stevie" strains
for me to win 40 cents

flat on his back
at the starting gate
the winner of 3000 races

racing form haiku:

"off slow
  closed well
  just missed"

her bright grey eyes
flash at me like the finish line photo
and the longest long shot rides in

cool

if by being cool you mean
10 below zero in february
standing on a street corner in the south bronx
trying to score heroin
a couple hundred black and puerto rican junkies
looking hard at you
the only white face there

or if by cool you mean
trapped and pinned
in a hell-hole roominghouse in toronto
2 psychotic men
press knives against your flesh
and one of them says
"I'm going to cut your throat"

or if the cops outside los angeles
have drawn their guns
pointed them at you
and the nastiest cop tells you
they are going to take you
into the desert
and shoot you
and no one will ever know

if by being cool you mean
situations like that
where you stay calm
make no false moves
and do not go
emotionally
around the bend into flip city

well
I have been cool in those circumstances
I survived

but if you mean
being cool
regarding me and you

well
I am afraid
I have no idea
what you are talking about

in this dangerous situation
in this passionate circumstance in vancouver
all I want to do
is scream out my feelings for you
like some
crazy-assed fool

who is anything
but cool

a true story

my cousin went away to a war /
and my uncle
was afraid his only son
whom he loved as much as he loved life itself
would be killed —
or wounded and maimed so badly
my cousin would no longer
be the son my uncle knew,
but someone else
alien to him /
a stranger

[handwritten: 신체상에 / permanently damaged]

[handwritten right margin: Emphasis on "killed" because Osborn skips to next line, when he could have continued to write on the same line.]

my uncle conceived tragic scenarios
day and night /
he worried so much he convinced himself
the chance his son would return to him was vanishing

[handwritten: imagined (above "conceived") and imagined (above "convinced")]

one afternoon my uncle walked to the barn
loaded his shotgun
and pulled the trigger /

my cousin came back from the war
without a scratch
and as intact as anyone can be

I know my uncle
I know him in my blood
I know him in my mind
I know him better and better

every hour she's gone

[handwritten: ? Irony? why "she"? what does "she" represent?]

one of them

I was always on the wrong side of the desk
in more trouble than anyone else
and certain the assholes I had to talk to
for food or a place to stay
had no idea
what
my life
was like

they had paycheques
cars
apartments
plenty of cigarettes
and someone keeping them warm

but then
I took this job
and hear my own words:

"you don't know what it's like!"

used on me

because I have control over beds and food
and can say
YES
or NO
to the desperate

bums
demanding cigarettes
like I have an endless supply

money
like I don't have rent to pay
or nights spent alone
broke and afraid

but they've been

drunk
drugged
rolled
or thrown out

and if I don't let them in
they'll break in somewhere
attack somebody
or kill themselves
they tell me

I have the keys in my hand now

but this guy comes in
big and stinking and wild-looking
the nuthouse kicked him into the streets
and he can't make it

he gets violent if he doesn't take his pills
and he doesn't
because they turn him into mush

it's early in the morning
with a hard autumn rain
coming
down
cold

I send him to the police station
for a ticket to stay at a mission
but he comes right back
so I call the desk sergeant and he says:

"they don't want him at the mission
the churches don't want him
and we don't want him
he's got mental problems
there's nothing we can do
he causes trouble
sorry"

I let him use the phone
until he starts calling people at random

he says he's been walking the streets
3 days and nights
no sleep
nothing to eat

I give him a bologna sandwich and cup of tomato juice
but since I decided he doesn't meet
the easily revised
ADMISSION CRITERIA
I tell him it's time to go

again
he tells me about his situation

"it's tough" I say
hustling him out the door

and he gives me a look that says
'you don't understand
or give a shit'

8 empty beds
a pot of coffee
a stack of sandwiches
still there after he heads down the street
into the rain
into the dark

I lock the door
sit down on the couch
light a cigarette
and read the paper

no problems

no problems at all

one of them

from the suicide ward

john my roommate tells me about being
over 60
no job
since he was fired
as maintenance man
from this same hospital

john grew up in an orphanage
shipped to sea
never married
said he never knew anything about it

john has just one room now
no money to go anywhere
nothing but
alcohol
pills
depression
overdoses
the same 4 walls
and heart trouble

"nothing to do" john says
hunches over his belly and cries

"I try to tell them" he sobs
"but they just don't understand"

deep

long

heart trouble

milton

milton my main man
used to sing with the dominoes
carry a gun
know sam cooke

milton helped save my life
saying hard truths
sticking by me

I think of him tonight
my heart's got a major gripe
I feel like stabbing god with a knife

but milton jumps into my head
and I can hear
what he always said
when I was twisted
and came to him
said "milton I got a problem"

and before I could wail the details
milton said

"lemme guess
  somebody ain't doin
  what you want em to do
  ain't that right?"

make me so mad
milton say that
forget other people
want to flatten
that milton cat

royalties

this wild friend of mine
a guy I've known for years
in the downtown eastside
reeled up to me in front of the ovaltine café

he said "how's your book of poetry doing?"

"well" I said "the first edition is selling out"

"you must be getting lots of royalties" he said
"so can you let me have a few bucks?"

"I owe my publisher money" I told him "I'm broke"

"you're kidding" my friend said

I shook my head

"then you're lying!"
and with that
he gave me a disgusted look
and spun out down the sidewalk

I was telling him the truth
my publisher fronts me copies of the book
and I'm supposed to pay him so much from each one I sell
but I end up spending all the money
so I owe him

and yesterday
when I went to see my publisher
to get some more books

Irony & Tone.

I went into his office
and he was sitting there looking lost and stunned
like he'd been on a drunk with a vampire
he had dark circles around his eyes
and bags beneath them as big as a full binner's sack

we went to an outdoor café
for a cup of coffee
I asked him how he was doing
and he actually told me
that's how bad he was feeling

he said he was broke
eating kraft dinner for days
turning 40 years old next week
just had a cyst removed from his balls
it hurt like hell down there
he could barely walk
his girlfriend had broken up with him
and he's been trying to drink it all away

I started laughing
I couldn't stop laughing
I never before felt so close to my publisher
I never before felt so much compassion for him

we were baking in the sun
drinking hot coffee
sweating
and he said "I don't care, take some more books"

I had a reading in burnaby last night
my publisher set it up
I sold 3 copies there
and promptly spent the 30 bucks on a good time

I learned from my grandfather
who always said
"I'd spend my last nickel on a good time"

but I thought of my poor publisher
and laughed
in misery's solidarity

after all
what other kind of publisher
should a poet of low-life trouble have
than mine?

and I was glad
that for once
I was the one
who paid for our coffee

outside at midnight

a young woman in a black party dress
at the intersection of east georgia and princess
staggers drunkenly
smashes an empty bottle in the street
then cries loudly in anguish:
"he's gone!
he's gone!
and it's all my fault!
I drove him away!
it's all my fault!"

I try to pass by her unnoticed
in the shadows on the sidewalk
but no   she sees me
and asks desperately:
"is that you?
is that you?"

"no" I say "it's not me"

"no" she says dejectedly "it's not you"

I walk quickly away
and am a block and a half from her
when I hear   an agonized scream:
"he's walking away!
come back!
please come back!"

I glance over my shoulder
she's lurching in my direction

and I think—

how like her we all are
lost
drunken
in darkness
with no one to comfort us
mistaking a passing shadow
for the one we are seeking
the one we have driven away
because of what we have done

outside

at midnight

where all our hope
is in her cries

hundred block rock

hundred block rock *a*
→ shoot up shock *a*
police chief *b*
cold grief *b*
war on drugs*c*
pull the plug *c*
clean it up *d*
nowhere to go *e*
ground zero *e*
overload jail *f*
rock and wail *f* —drug addict
where a (dopefiend) stood *g*
comin soon *h*
to your neighbourhood *g*

knock it down *a*
up or down *a*
crack packers
jacked up
"empty your pockets"
say the cops
(the bug) is loose
sellin juice — 도시집없이
(suburban) kids
come to use
hundred block rock

blue eagle cafe
hotel balmoral
blood stains
illegal
latino
black
aboriginal
white
trash
flashin cash
smashin locks
no detox
hundred block rock

need a place
say the faces
keith
senior citizen
leanin and dealin
flyin and dyin
welfare bribe situation

blue teardrop tattoos
what's the plan
tear it down
let 'em drown
too much reality
fixin in the alley
blood streamin
naked girl tweakin
hundred block reelin
vancouver's first
western world's worst
hiv
public health emergency
fuck 'em around
till their lives burst

media deluge
  flesh scenes
    teevee schemes
      want to see
        somebody fix
          hustle tricks
            die with no place
              to take a shit
                killed by politics

people stare
  get shocked
    afraid they do
      hundred block rock
        john popped
          ppt
            ain't no big dealer
              ain't no
                burma opium cia trafficker
                  just native
                    poor
                      positive
                        scufflin hard
                          can't go too far
                            nobody gonna rescue
                              underclass fools

sirens
  screams
    abandon these
    abandon you
      got threes
        got vees
          the bug is loose
            canada goose
              cooked
                hundred block truth

somebody's baby
  from the fraser valley
    the bible belt
      ain't no help
        jesus bleedin
          weepin
            dyin in shock
              jesus doin
                hundred block rock

let dopefiends die
  but don't call it
    genocide
      no place to hide
        kick in the door
          nothin but whores
            stick your badge
              right up their ass
                stinkin shit hole
                  hundred block hotel
                    gonna replace
                      disgrace
                        with tourists
up or down

up or down
  see the alien clown
    in the doorway
      on the bus bench
        sold the rent cheque
        (forlorn creature) — 거울 보고, 자신 못 날아 보기
        soul mirror
          o.d. on the corner
          cop some blow
            blow some cop
              chicken in the alley
                hundred block rock

vilify ··· 나쁘게 말하다
  isolate
    incarcerate — keep in prison / other place
      decimate — 많은 사람들을 죽이다 //
        don't forget
          hundred block rock
          illegal
          latino
            black
              aboriginal
              white
              trash
                hundred block

(crash)

see my face

I walk to a 24-hour corner store
east hastings and gore
12:30 in the morning
the air is raw
a hooker inside the place says
"can you buy me a cigarette?"

I do
and she tries to give me some change
I say "you asked me to buy it for you
        it's yours"

"thanks" she says and adds
"I got attacked tonight
  see my face"

she pushes back long brown strands of hair
"two women jumped me"

I look at
the wounds
and blood
across her cheek and nose and ear and neck

"my old man was there" she says
"and he ran off and left me
  he ran off with all my rent money
  now I'm homeless
  thanks for the cigarette"

and she walks away

the hebrews said you could not look
on the face of god
and live

but if you could
I think god's face
would look a lot
like hers

legacy

my mother served in the united states army
so whenever her
later visionary adventures
crashed and burned
she'd be eligible to retreat
to a veterans' administration
psychiatric ward
and rekindle
the next manic illuminations
by which her life
was increasingly guided

and she would always be placed
(for reasons I could never quite understand)
in a ward with
stressed-out and addicted
male vietnam veterans
many of whom
grew quite fond of her
and waited on her night and day
yeah she'd be
the only female patient there

one afternoon
I received a phone call
after she'd been
locked up long enough
to envision her next undertaking
and a tremendous one it was
she declared to me
very excitedly
that she was going to run

in the upcoming election
for president of the united states

perhaps you can imagine
your mother
saying such a thing
but saying it and meaning it
really are
two different experiences

anyway
I am sure I replied noncommittally
"oh yeah?"
hoping to let it go at that
but my mother rushed on
"yes!" she exclaimed
"I think I have a real good chance too!"
"oh yeah?"
"yes!" she said decisively
"I should be able
to get all the votes
from alcoholics
drug addicts
mental patients
vietnam vets
how can I lose?"
"gee ma" I said
"sounds like a sure thing to me"

"so bud" she said
"what I want you to do
is think about which cabinet post you want
how about that!"

well
in my family
if we didn't count our chickens
long before they'd hatched
I don't think we'd have been able
to do very much
counting at all
so I told my mother
I would definitely
think about it

but then she told me
she was on her way out of the hospital
and had already
scheduled a press conference
at a downtown hotel
to announce her candidacy

'uh oh' I thought 'this could be . . .'
who the hell ever knew
what anything could become
besides more trouble?

"it's always something"
my grandmother edna
my mother's mother
used to say
"it's always something"

well
being a drug addict
an alcoholic
and having only recently
come out of a nuthouse myself
and working my way

rapidly
towards jail
I saw I had a lot to offer
my mother's administration
and as I didn't see anything else I could do
I spent considerable time
trying to decide
between
secretary of health education and welfare
where I'd raise social assistance
to the level of income
of corporate ceos
and make all the universities and health care
free
or secretary of defense
and send the u.s. army marines navy and air force
against shell oil
itt
the cia
the international monetary fund
the trilateral commission
etc
etc

you can tell from this
that I have always been a big help
during family crises
but my sister
after receiving her phone call
from our mother
knew exactly what to do

my sister has put out more fires
set by members of our family
who blaze like arsonists

through each others' lives
than the fire station at main and powell
in the downtown eastside
puts out in one year

so after confirming
a press conference
had indeed been set up
and a multitude of local media
were preparing to descend
and record
our mother's campaign announcement
my sister contacted the media
and suggested that maybe
waiting a little while
to see how things developed
would be the best
tact to take
seeing as how our mother
was just now
leaving a psych ward
against her psychiatrist's advice
and did not seem
to have a firm grasp
on the rigours involved
in being a presidential candidate
and I agreed
to support
my sister's action

but looking back
years later
I must say
and I'm sure my sister
would agree

considering
how horribly
everything turned out anyway
allowing the press conference
to proceed
could have meant
another authentic highlight
amidst the low-life
brilliance
of our family history

and today I truly appreciate
my own mother
at least
dared
what other would-be political leaders
run like hell away from
and that is
seeking elected office
the presidency no less
on behalf
of the last
the lowest
the worst
the left-out
those who are freezing
or starving
or crazy
or addicted
or abandoned
on the streets
and in the institutions
of the united states of america

wow

man
the things that can happen to you
all in one lifetime

yesterday
I was a burned-out junkie on the corner
main and hastings
today
I wake up in the strong and slender arms
of a beautiful young woman

yesterday
I woke up alone
in a pile of ashes and rags and sick sweat
yesterday
I was in a shit-hole s.r.o.
cockroaches and spiders and mice
yesterday
I woke up and looked through a dirty little window
at a blank wall

today
I wake up and see mountains and city skyline
through wall-sized windows wide open
today
I live in a large clean apartment
on the 6th floor of social housing
and instead of like
yesterday
when I woke up looking
into empty dope bags and empty pill bottles
today

I look into her eyes
which even the glorious shades of light
in the vancouver sky
do not contain

yesterday
I woke up so malnourished
I could've slashed my wrists
on sharp and jutting pelvic bones
today
she lightly strokes my chest and my bulging belly
and our first kiss of the day
goes on for hours

yesterday
when I got up
I thieved and conned and deceived
just to get for myself
and got hold of nothing but trouble
but today
when I give all
of what little I've got left of myself
I receive unexpected and abundant
blessings and gifts of kindnesses

yesterday
when I was a junkie on the corner
I woke up and didn't want
to hear anything or feel anything or touch anything
today
I wake up
and feel her breath on my face
I feel her skin
like lightly perfumed silk next to mine

but man
when you wake up
from living death
and open yourself up
and open your life up
and your heart too
and go out on all the limbs you can climb out on
and when you lay yourself wide open
to a beautiful young woman
and you're a beat-up old man
man
you got all the trouble you can handle

it ain't junkie-on-the-corner-dying-in-the-street
kind of trouble
but you're shooting rapids without an oar
without even a canoe
man you're drowning
in the sea of love

I love the geese flying over the rooftops
I love the seagulls swooping past
I love the sparrows bopping around
and I love the blue sky
I love the sunlight on green leaves
I love the mountains that are almost transparent light-blue
I even love the cars
no
I don't love the death machines on the georgia viaduct
but they're there anyway

man o man
I'm living right now
and I'm dying right now
I'm scared and crazy and mangled and battered

I'm broken and my blood has been spilled
spilled through all the years
and all the streets
and all the nights
but somehow
this woman is absolutely beaming at me

the first thing she told me was
"I'm probably going to break your heart"
o shit
what I spent all those years
a junkie   a wino   a suicide
trying to prevent
my heart has been a monolithic barricade
you couldn't get next to me with a knife at my throat
or especially with love coming close
no way
but today
forget about it
I'm wide open
take your shot

she says
"you've got scars all over your head"
man
I have fractured and cracked my head so hard so often
how can I even be here?
even semi-coherent?
without a clue most of the time
about what the fuck to do?
just here
and man
I love
my heart is out there
yesterday I was full of hate
but today I love

I love all the poets and all the poems
I love to move my hand slowly through her hair
I love the way the sunlight touches
her golden brown strands
I love to kiss
her throat and her breasts and her legs
and her mouth and her arms and her stomach
I love to kiss and caress
every centimetre
every millimetre
every molecule
man
I love every song sam cooke and wilson pickett ever sang

I feel like I'm getting killed
here's my heart
and o lord will I ever be singing the blues soon
"soon" she said
look out baby
"you sure are grateful" she said to me
grateful?
are you kidding?
am I grateful?
I could soar into the sky
on the mightiest eagle wings
of gratitude
and whip under the lions gate bridge
and swoop over the lions
and even spin the woodward's sign around in a time or 2
my heart is being reborn

and I am a fool
an old fool
yesterday I was a junkie on the corner
stuck in the street

today I am being dribbled like a basketball
by a beautiful young woman
because I don't know nothing about women
man
talk about homicide or suicide
or being locked up in the nuthouse
or burned out in the streets and shit
I've got a clue
but am I grateful?
yesterday
I was the most miserable man who ever drew breath
today
there cannot be a happier man in vancouver
no way
today
I am the happiest man in vancouver

and I am in disbelief
what with the kind of life and kind of attitude I've had
to say that I am
the happiest man in vancouver
at this moment
because I know nobody can be happier than this
and live
well
I am truly in shock
you can't imagine
I couldn't imagine
today
from yesterday

and man o man
if I am still here tomorrow
and she's long gone
I won't be doggoned

my heart will still be out there
hurting   crying   singing   flying
no shit?
no shit
man
there she is
calling me on the phone again
what's wrong with that woman?

man
this is a strange life
a strange world
and I am ready to go elsewhere
I could die right now
but not from sorrow
I could die from joy
but otherwise
if I'm here
no matter what crap is coming down
no matter how many pieces my heart is in
I will be sitting on the wing
of a big beautiful bird flying straight and true
towards those
almost transparent light-blue mountains
right out
there

wow

complaint of an advocate

sad, lord
tired and worn
and sick
so sick
of power politics
of turf wars
of meetings and committees and subcommittees
sick of everything that loses
focus
because every deception
every agenda
every meeting
every resentment
every control grab
every move for the money
slams down hardest
on the most wretched human beings
in north america
who are suffering and dying
in the streets and alleys and shit-hole hotels
of the downtown eastside
all the pettiness and ambition
slams directly down
on those who are most afflicted
by poverty and illness
addiction and discrimination
homelessness and demonizing propaganda
so, lord
I want to quit
I want to stop
I want to say fuck it
it's too fucking hard

I am old and beat and hurt like a bastard
I want to sit beneath a tree
a dog beside me
the ocean in front of me
and write an occasional haiku
about a passing cloud
I feel like hell
my life is a mess
I can't sleep worth a damn
my health is shot
I keep going by consuming
caffeine and sugar and nicotine and aspirins
I have no paid job and no resources
to deal
with all this shit
the agencies
the bureaucracies
the manoeuvering for advantage
all the greed and fear
the loss of focus
but I remember
(and this is why memory is such a liability
to self-interest)
I remember her eyes
glistening with tears
in the lobby of the pacific cinematheque
after the showing
of her documentary
tu as crie / let me go
a long beautiful love poem
to her daughter
a heroin addict
and prostitute
murdered in montreal
her film also

a plea
a challenge
to transcend
the senseless and bankrupt slaughter
of the war on drugs
so yeah
today when I feel like shit
and want to quit
I see her eyes
glistening with tears
after I held up for her
that day's vancouver sun
with the headline
western world's worst
hiv/aids epidemic among drug users
in the downtown eastside
she said
don't stop fighting
she looked directly into my eyes and said
don't stop fighting
and today
when the fight seems too fierce to deal with
when it feels like it's killing me
I remember her eyes
I hear her words
and I remember
this junkie in the downtown eastside
who has aids
and who came up to me recently
after our dopefiend discussion meeting
where we discussed
fighting towards a life-saving
and enlightened place
he'd been very articulate during the meeting
he understands the situation

in his flesh
in his misery
in his anger
he understands
how other people hate him
and wish he'd just
go away somewhere out of sight
and die
he said to me
you know how cynical I am
about anything good
happening for us
but this meeting today
it gives me
a ray of hope
and I see his face
illuminated for a moment
with that most alien and elusive
expression
hope
today
when I feel hopeless
when the odds are too long
the deck stacked against
the clock running out
and who the fuck am I anyway?
a junkie myself
a fucking mental case
surviving on social assistance
straight just a few years
and ripped again
with dopefiend cravings
for pain relief
shit
sitting in meetings

with people paid to be there
and I pass up the fucking sandwich lines
to sit and listen to them
and get frustrated and pissed off
and hungry and depressed
shit
and then I see her eyes
and hear her voice
and see on his anguished face
a ray of hope
and then I walk
past the walton and the patricia hotels
within a block of each other
in the downtown eastside
and see the first names of my father and mother
both of whom died homeless and broke
my father full of drugs and booze
when he hanged himself in jail
and my mother
wracked by drug addiction
and mental illness
whose friends at the end
were crackheads and thieves
walton and patricia
and remember
how my parents were
jailed
and scapegoated
but I still want to say fuck it
I don't have to do this
I'm not strung-out now
I've gotten a miracle pass to a new life
why waste it down here
in this mess of shit and trouble
where I've spent

nearly all of my fucking life
I could hustle something better
than stretching between
the gutter with the scum
and meeting rooms
with lying backstabbing sleight-of-hand bureaucratic hustlers
yeah I remember
my father got rid of all our furniture
except for the beds
because he said furniture
was too middle-class
so no I'm not too happy
with all this
manipulating glad-ass convivial crap
dehumanizing me even further
but I remember
reading about
the first dirt-poor black man
sprung from an alabama death row
for a murder he didn't commit
sprung largely
through the intense and tenacious efforts
of a young black lawyer
with a graduate degree from harvard law
who could've written his own ticket
to corporate law firms coast to coast
but chose to defend
for almost nothing
the baddest and most undeserving of poor people
and this lawyer
defines the role of an advocate
by telling a bible story
when jesus came upon some men
fixing to stone to death
a woman who violated their morality

and jesus told them
to let the man who never fucked up
throw the first stone
and the men became ashamed of themselves
dropped their stones
and walked home
but this young black lawyer
says that kind of thing
wouldn't work now
because people today
not only don't become ashamed of themselves
but are only too eager to decide
who will live
and who will die
and so an advocate today
says the lawyer
an advocate today
must be
a stone catcher
catching stones
with your nerves
your heart
your skin
your life
catching stones intended for those like
the western world's worst
for those like
my father and mother
today
when I don't feel I can take
another moment of it
when I don't want to take
anymore of it
when I think I must be a complete fool
to go through another day of it

when today
hits me so goddamned hard
then the fight that is in my blood
the ray of hope that is in my soul
the high threshold for pain burned into my bones
remembers
despite myself
who I am
and where I stand
when the stones
are being
thrown
who I am
and where I stand
when the stones
are being
thrown